JASPER
& SCRUFF

*For my
very supportive
parents and
husband Gavin*

Praise for *Jasper & Scruff*:

"...a wonderfully warm
and funny book"
Irish Independent

"...a hilarious story of
friendship and what
really matters, packed
with laugh-aloud
humour"
Parents in Touch

STRIPES PUBLISHING
LIMITED
An imprint of
the Little Tiger Group
1 Coda Studios
189 Munster Road,
London SW6 6AW

A paperback original
First published
in Great Britain in 2019

Text and illustrations copyright
© Nicola Colton, 2019

ISBN: 978-1-78895-053-4

The right of Nicola Colton to be
identified as the author and illustrator
of this work has been asserted by her
in accordance with the Copyright,
Designs and Patents Act, 1988.

Printed and bound in China.

STP/1800/0268/0519

2 4 6 8 10 9 7 5 3 1

Nicola Colton

JASPER
& SCRUFF

HUNT
for the
GOLDEN
BONE

stripes

Jasper was the type of
cat who liked the finer
things in life. Fancy meals,
bow ties and collecting art.

His best friend Scruff liked the simpler things. Chasing his ball, sniffing out adventures and anything salted caramel flavour.

Jasper was also the type of cat who had always dreamed of running a bookshop.

And now he did ...
with the help of Scruff.

SPOOKY SECTION

SPY SECTION

ANTIQUES SECTION

CHILDREN'S SECTION

BESTSELLERS

THE MOG & MUTT

THE MOG & MUTT

One morning, Jasper was counting the money in the till as they waited for the first customers of the day.

"Scruff, I think we've sold even more books than last week," he purred contentedly. "Scruff?"

"Wheeeeee!" cried Scruff, as he slid past on a rolling ladder, knocking some books to the floor.

Jasper sighed as he went to pick them up. He had asked Scruff to dust the shelves, but he didn't mean like that!

Ting-a-ling!

A bell rang as the shop door swung open.

"Be with you in just a minute,"
Jasper called.

A hooded figure tiptoed across
the floor and placed a package
lightly on the counter.

Ting-a-ling!

The bell tinkled again as the figure left.
Jasper turned round.

"Scruff," he said, looking down at the
parcel. "Did you see who left this?"

"Wheeeeee!" Scruff whizzed past again.

Jasper carefully tore open the paper
to reveal a leather-bound book.

"Black Whiskers," he said, tracing his
paw over the fancy lettering on the cover.

Scruff leaped down from the ladder
and skidded across the counter.

"The pirate?" he panted.

"Ugh! You're getting drool on my bow tie," groaned Jasper, dabbing at it with his hanky.

"Go on! What does it say?" asked Scruff.

Jasper opened the book and began to read.

Black Whiskers was Captain of the *Silver Sardine*. A skilled treasure hunter, she discovered riches all over the world. It was said that she used up most of her nine lives battling storms and fighting sea monsters. She set out on her last voyage to Dogtooth Island in search of the legendary Golden Bone. But she never returned...

"Wow!" said Scruff, his tail wagging. "I heard that her first mate stole the Golden Bone."

As Jasper turned the page, a yellowing sheet of paper floated to the ground.

"Look!" yapped Scruff. "A treasure map."

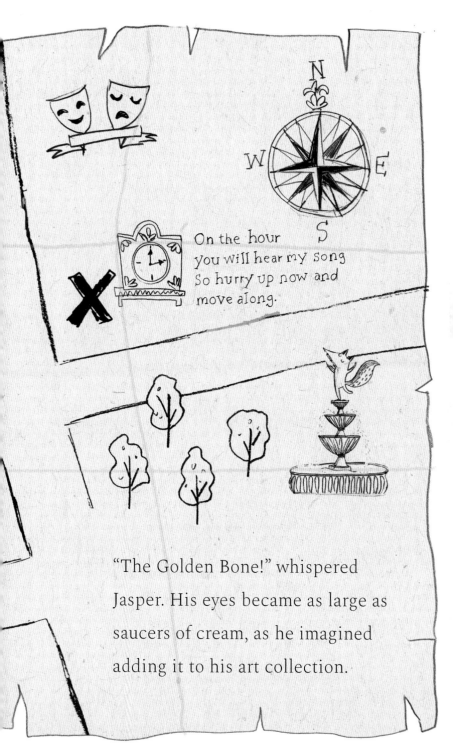

On the hour
you will hear my song
So hurry up now and
move along.

"The Golden Bone!" whispered
Jasper. His eyes became as large as
saucers of cream, as he imagined
adding it to his art collection.

But as Jasper picked up the map, Scruff grabbed the other end between his teeth.

"Grrrr," growled the puppy playfully.
Tug of war was one of his favourite games!

"Scruff, let go. You're going to tear it," said Jasper.

Riiiiiiip!

Jasper stumbled backwards into a display of books. "Ow!" he yelped.

"Ack!" spluttered Scruff, coughing up a piece of the map.

Jasper smoothed out the crumpled map on the counter. Then he picked up the soggy scrap with his hanky and put it in its place.

"It looks like a map of our town," said Jasper, twiddling his whiskers thoughtfully. "But how could the Golden Bone have ended up here?"

Jasper fetched his magnifying glass to take a closer look. "Ah, there's something written beside Mrs Caw's clock shop," he said. "It could be a clue. *On the hour you will hear my song. So hurry up now and move along.*"

"It's almost ten o'clock now,"
said Scruff. "Let's go!"

"What about the shop?"
asked Jasper.

"Oh, come on. It'll be fun!" said Scruff.
"I'll make a sign to let everyone know
we'll be back soon."

"Hmmm, I suppose..." said Jasper.

"Yay! An adventure! I love adventures," said
Scruff, as he ducked behind the counter.

A few minutes later, he reappeared waving a sign and wearing a large hat.

"Er, Scruff ... what's that?"

"It's my pirate hat. Do you like it?" Scruff said. "I've even managed to tuck my treasure-hunting kit inside."

"It's certainly, um … interesting,"

said Jasper.

As Scruff hung his sign on the door,
Jasper looked for the key to lock up the
shop. But it wasn't in its usual spot.

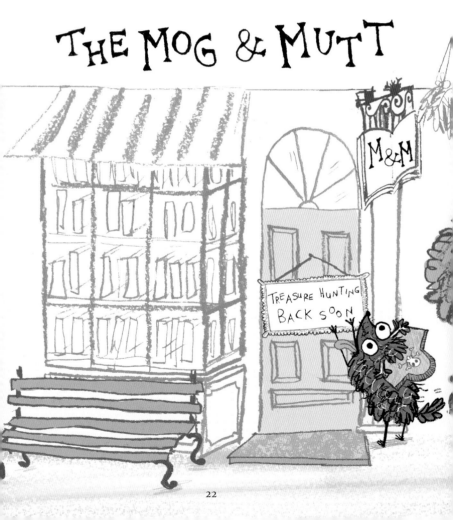

THE MOG & MUTT

M&M

TREASURE HUNTING
BACK SOON

"Scruff, did you move the key?"
he asked.

Scruff shook his head.

"Never mind," said Jasper, plucking a
spare key from under a plant pot.

There was no time to lose, so the pair
took a shortcut through the park.
As they got closer to Mrs Caw's
shop, they could hear music.

CLICK
CLICK

ALVIS
PAWSLEY

"Morning, Mrs Caw," said Scruff,
bounding inside.

"Shoopy dooby do, you're my weekend
bird..." crowed Mrs Caw, as she
polished a display case.

Jasper clicked along to the music.
Alvis Pawsley was his favourite singer.

"Do you have any clocks that sing
on the hour?" asked Scruff.

"Oh, hello there," said Mrs Caw,
turning down the record player.
"A clock with some flowers, you say?"

"Er, no, a clock that sings on the
hour," repeated Jasper.

"Sings? Hmm..." said Mrs Caw, resting her beak on her wing. "We've got Tickers and Tockers, Chimers and Buzzers, Dingers and Dongers, but no singing clocks. We do have one that goes—"

Cuckoo!

Jasper almost jumped out of his fur.

"Yes, that's the one," said Mrs Caw,
pointing up at a cuckoo clock.

"Look, something just fell out of the
cuckoo's beak," said Scruff.

"You don't mind if we take that,
do you?" asked Jasper.

Outside, Jasper unfolded
the piece of paper.

I'm as salty as the sea,
but sweet as cake.
Eat me too fast
and you'll get a headache.

"Mmmm, I know this one!" Scruff
licked his lips. "It's got to be Salty
Cyril's salted caramel ice cream."

"Really?" said Jasper. "Are you sure?"
This clue seemed a little easy.

"If I'm wrong, we can still
have ice cream!" said Scruff.

"All right then," said Jasper.

"But Salty Cyril's is miles away."

"Why don't we ask Mrs Caw if we can borrow her tandem?" suggested Scruff.

They cycled across town to
Snootington-on-Sea. Jasper did
most of the work as Scruff's paws
could only just reach the pedals.

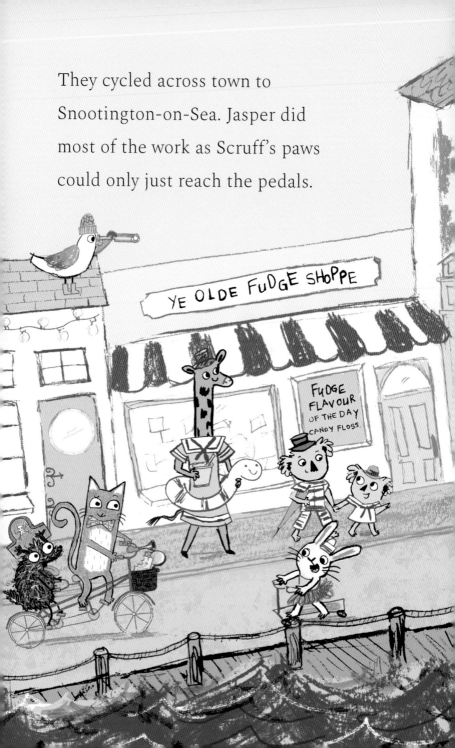

YE OLDE FUDGE SHOPPE

FUDGE
FLAVOUR
OF THE DAY
CANDY FLOSS.

SALLY'S SEASIDE SHOP

Out of breath, Jasper stopped by a
cheerily painted boat tied to the pier,
beside a large wooden ice-cream cone.

"Ahoy, me hearties. What can I get ye
on this fine day?" asked Salty Cyril,
leaning out of a porthole.

"We'll take all of your salted caramel ice cream, please," said Scruff.

"ALL of it?" asked Salty Cyril.

"Yes, ALL of it, please," said Jasper. "And two spoons."

The pair ate

and ate

and ate.

Finally, they reached the bottom
of the tub. Jasper's head throbbed
and his tummy ached.

"What if we *never* find the
Golden Bone?" he groaned.

But Scruff wasn't listening.
Buzzing from all the sugar, he zipped
around in circles chasing his ball.

The ball knocked into the wooden
cone. It wobbled and then...

Ker-*thunk!*

The wooden cone tipped over and the scoop of ice cream bounced away.

Something was taped to the inside of the cone. Scruff picked it up with his teeth and dropped it into Jasper's lap.

"Eww!" said Jasper.
"It's covered in drool!"

"It's a key!" said Scruff. "Maybe it opens a treasure chest."

"And look, there's another clue," said Jasper. "Do you mind if we take this, Cyril?"

"Not at all," replied Cyril. "Ye 'ave just bought a week's worth o' ice cream. I be happy to help."

Jasper read the clue:

A place of curtains, lights and magic,
For those who enjoy all things dramatic
Tread the boards until they squeak,
You will find the treasure that your seek.

"Lights, curtains, drama..." said Jasper.
"I know this one. It has to be the
Velvet Theatre!" He even knew a way
to get in from his acting days.
"You were right, Scruff. This is fun!
Now, let's get back on that bike."

Before long they arrived at the theatre.
Jasper leaned the tandem against
a lamp post and led the way round
the back. He pulled away some ivy
to reveal a door.

Jasper stepped inside and reached
for a switch on the wall. *Click!*

A bright spotlight illuminated the stage.
They stepped out from the wings.

"We need to find the squeak," said
Scruff, jumping on the wooden boards.
He stomped up and down until...

Eeeeeee! a floorboard whined.

"That's it!" cried Jasper, his tail
flicking back and forth with
excitement.

Scruff sniffed around. "There's a
handle here," he said. "Help me pull!"

They pulled and pulled
and finally it gave way.

"A trap door!" they said together,
peering into the darkness below.

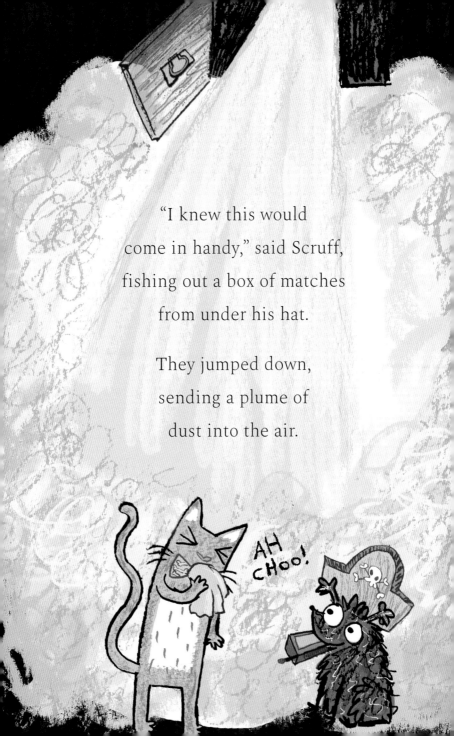

"I knew this would
come in handy," said Scruff,
fishing out a box of matches
from under his hat.

They jumped down,
sending a plume of
dust into the air.

AH
CHOO!

As Jasper lit a match, Scruff ran on ahead.

The puppy stopped by a pile of masks
and bejewelled costumes. He then
started to try things on.

Look at me!" he said, twirling in a circle.

"The treasure could be just around the corner, Scruff," said Jasper, rolling his eyes. "You can play dress-up later."

"I suppose so," said Scruff, stuffing some costumes under his hat.

Jasper lit another match.
He spotted a large wooden treasure
chest with a gold trim.

"That has to be it!" he said, hurrying
over. Scruff skidded to a halt beside him
and passed him the key.

Jasper slid the key into the lock and
turned it carefully. Then he lifted the lid.

Creeeak!

Holding his breath, Scruff
peered inside. But it was empty
except for a slip of paper.

"Oh, not another clue,"
moaned Jasper. "We really do
need to get back to the shop."

He lit another match
and read it out:

Look Up

Three hooded figures loomed through
the trapdoor above them.

"Who are you?" Jasper demanded.

"Grrrrrrr!" growled Scuff,
baring his teeth.

"Hello, darlings,"
trilled a familiar voice.

"Lady Catterly!" Jasper hissed, as the
figure lowered her hood.

The other figures lowered
their hoods too.

"Reginald and Oswald!" barked Scruff.

"And here we leave you two alone,
because there is no Golden Bone!"
squealed Lady Catterly.

The Sophisticats grinned down at them.
Then the trapdoor slammed shut.

"Nooooo!" howled Scruff.

"We're trapped," muttered Jasper. *The*
Sophisticats must've hatched this plan to get
revenge for my dinner party, he reflected.
After all, they did end up eating cake
covered in puppy hair and drool.

The last match burned out and the pair
were plunged into inky blackness.

Jasper tried to think of
an escape plan... But the
trapdoor was too high up.

"I smell hot dogs," said
Scruff, interrupting
Jasper's thoughts.

"Hot dogs?" said Jasper.
"How can you think of
your stomach, Scruff?
We have to find a way out."

But Scruff scurried off.

"Here!" said the puppy. He nudged the back wall and a panel fell open.

"Well done, Scruff!" Jasper cried.

They squeezed through the gap and found themselves in a metal pipe.

"I think we're in an air vent,"
said Jasper. "Just follow your nose."

They crawled along and then
climbed upwards until...

"I *see* hot dogs!" barked Scruff,
as he reached a grill.

He pushed it open and tumbled out into
the lobby, right in front of a hot-dog seller.

Jasper was close behind.

"Thank goodness!" he said, dusting himself
down and straightening his bow tie.

"Two hot dogs, please,"
said Scruff to the hot-dog seller.

Scruff gulped down his hot dog
happily, while Jasper picked at his
with a knife and fork.

"Now, can we get back to the bookshop?" said Jasper, handing the rest of his hot dog to Scruff.

"Yum! More for me!" said Scruff, as he followed Jasper outside.

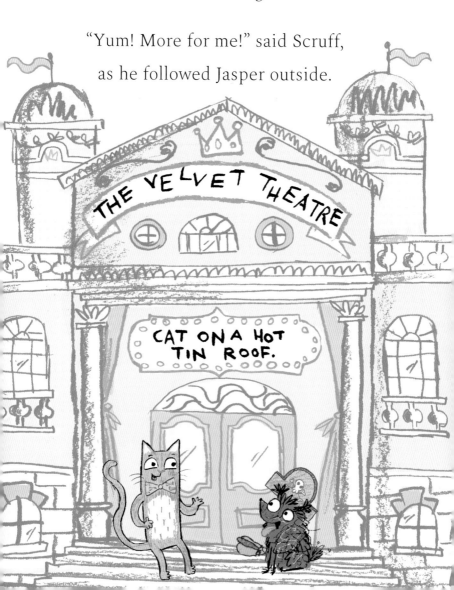

THE VELVET THEATRE

CAT ON A HOT
TIN ROOF.

The town clock chimed three
as they reached the Mog and Mutt.

Jasper was just about to unlock
the door when a dark shadow
fell over him.

They looked up to see
two enormous gorillas.

"It seems you are trespassing,"
said one.

"Trespassing?" said Jasper,
raising an eyebrow. "This is our shop,
I'll have you know."

GRRRRR

"I think you'll find it's under new ownership," said the other gorilla, pointing at the window.

Inside, Lady Catterly sat with her feet propped on the counter, a key dangling from a chain around her neck.

Oswald was chewing toffee and leafing through a book with his sticky paws.

Reginald poked at a display with his umbrella, knocking some books to the floor.

Jasper let out a groan. *So that's why they tricked us. They wanted our shop!*

"We'd best be sending you on your way," the gorillas said together.

Jasper and Scruff were lifted high in the air and landed in a heap in the gutter.

Head spinning, Jasper sat up
slowly to see a pair of boots with
shiny buckles in front of him.
A gloved paw helped him to his feet.

"It seems we have something
in common," said the cat in
a voice as velvet as her hat.
"Lady Catterly has stolen from us."

"Black Whiskers!"

exclaimed Scruff, getting to his feet.

"I thought you were lost at sea,"
said Jasper.

"I was. I sailed on three different
ships, on seven different seas, to make
it back here. Is there somewhere we
can talk?" the pirate asked.

Back at Jasper and Scruff's apartment,
over steaming mugs of Catnip tea,
Black Whiskers explained how she and
Lady Catterly had once been friends.

"I loved discovering new lands," said
the pirate. "While Lady Catterly loved
shopping for precious spices,
silk and jewellery."

"Then we heard about the
treasure on Dogtooth Island."
Her green eyes narrowed.

"It was protected by a giant octopus,"
Black Whiskers went on, adjusting
the sword on her belt. "I battled the
creature and won, of course."

"But while I was busy fighting,
Lady Catterly stole the Golden Bone
and sailed away with my ship!"

"So Lady Catterly has the Golden Bone?" gasped Scruff.

Black Whiskers nodded. "Yes, I've heard that she wears it to special events."

"Well then," said Jasper, opening his notebook. "I have a plan."

Later that day, an invitation arrived at
The Sophisticats' headquarters.

Intimate concert with

Alvis Pawsley at

exclusive new venue:

The Gilded Kipper

Snootington-on-Sea pier

7pm

Only the

most fabulous

allowed admission

RSVP

"I suppose we can make an appearance," Lady Catterly purred.

Reginald and Oswald nodded.

"The Sophisticats expect the full V.I.P. treatment, of course," she added.

That evening, disguised in the theatre costumes, Jasper and Scruff watched through a porthole as The Sophisticats arrived. As Lady Catterly walked up the red carpet to *The Gilded Kipper*, something glittered between her ears.

"The Golden Bone!" Scruff nudged Jasper. "It's on Lady Catterly's tiara."

"A fishing boat, how quaint," said Lady Catterly, stepping aboard. "I've been on far more impressive vessels on my travels."

The Gilded Kipper

"Seen it before," said Reginald, yawning.

"I hope there's food,"
said Oswald, licking his lips.

As Salty Cyril steered the boat out
to sea, Jasper served drinks while
Scruff handed out canapés.

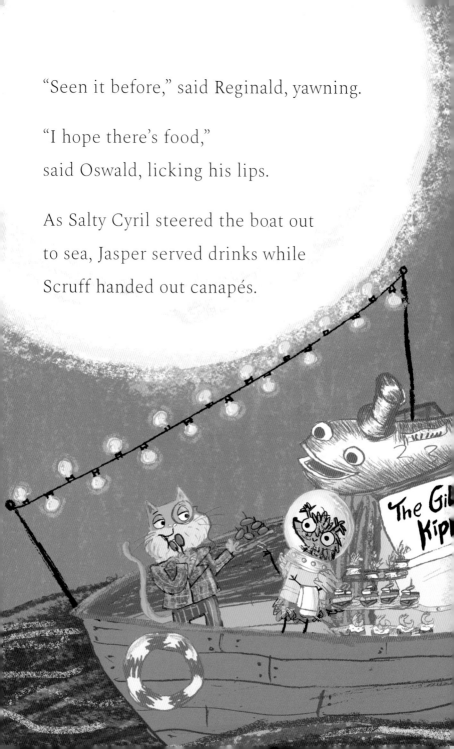

"What are we waiting for?"
whined Lady Catterly.
"We want Alvis!"

"Alvis! Alvis!" shouted Reginald.

"The cocktail sausages have run out!"
grumbled Oswald.

"If you'll kindly come this way,
I will now take you to see Alvis," Jasper
said. "You just need to walk across here."
He gestured to a narrow plank of wood.

"This is outrageous!"
yowled Lady Catterly.

"It's awfully dark," said Oswald.

"I'm not sure about this,"
muttered Reginald.

"All part of the surprise," said Jasper.
"We've just arrived at a private island
for the concert."

"Well, it does sound exclusive," said
Lady Catterly, brightening.

The Sophisticats reached the
end of the plank.

"I don't see an island..." said Lady
Catterly uneasily. "Just water."

"Yes," said Black Whiskers, leaping
out of the shadows. "There is an island
nearby but you'll have to swim for it."

"YOU!" shrieked Lady Catterly.
"What are YOU doing here?"

"Nice to see you too, old friend.
Before you go, I'll take this."

The pirate lifted the key from Lady
Catterly's neck with a flick of her sword.

Swish!

"And my treasure," Black Whiskers
added, snatching the tiara from
Lady Catterly's head.

Startled, Lady Catterly fell backwards,
pulling Reginald and Oswald with her.

Splash!

The three cats flailed about in the water.

Jasper and Scruff removed their
disguises and waved down at them.
"See you later!" they called.

"We'll get you for this!"
screeched Lady Catterly.

As the friends sailed back to shore,
they could hear the howls of
The Sophisticats on the wind.

The next day, Jasper and Scruff held a grand reopening party at the Mog and Mutt.

As guest of honour, Black Whiskers thrilled everyone with tales of her adventures at sea.

Alvis Pawsley sang some of
his greatest hits.

Salty Cyril served his
famous ice cream.

It was a wonderful evening.
The whole town was invited,
apart from three snooty cats.

Jasper went to find Scruff. "Time to crack open the Sparkling Catnip Juice, I think. That was a lot of fun, even though it didn't go quite as planned. I hope we can go on more adventures together."

"Yes! Me too!" said Scruff, wagging his tail.